AMANDINA

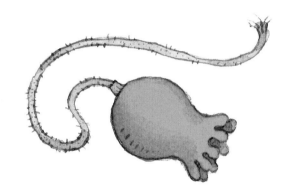

SERGIO RUZZIER

A NEAL PORTER BOOK
ROARING BROOK PRESS
NEW YORK

For Frances Foster

Copyright © 2008 by Sergio Ruzzier
A Neal Porter Book
Published by Roaring Brook Press
Roaring Brook Press is a division of Holtzbrinck Publishing Holdings Limited Partnership
175 Fifth Avenue, New York, New York 10010
www.roaringbrookpress.com

Distributed in Canada by H. B. Fenn and Company, Ltd.

Library of Congress Cataloging-in-Publication Data
Ruzzier, Sergio.
Amandina / Sergio Ruzzier. — 1st ed.
p. cm.
Summary: Amandina decides to overcome her shyness and show the town what a talented little dog she is, but when no one shows up for her performance, she finds that she also has a lot of perseverance.
"A Neal Porter book."
ISBN-13: 978-1-59643-236-9 ISBN-10: 1-59643-236-5
[1. Dogs—Fiction. 2. Bashfulness—Fiction. 3. Persistence—Fiction.] I. Title.
PZ7.R9475Am 2008 [E]—dc22 2007047914

Roaring Brook Press books are available for special promotions and premiums.
For details, contact: Director of Special Markets, Holtzbrinck Publishers.

Printed in China
First edition September 2008
2 4 6 8 10 9 7 5 3 1

Amandina Goldeneyes was taking her daily walk on the waterfront. She was, as usual, all alone.

Amandina was a wonderful little dog: she could dance, and sing, and act beautifully, and perform the most daring acrobatics. But nobody knew that, because nobody knew Amandina.

That evening, she promised herself that she would stop being so shy.

And so, she decided to give a great performance and invite everyone.

She rented a run-down theater in the old town. It needed some repairs, here and there, but that was not a problem, because Amandina was also very handy.

The very next day, she made a list of all the things she needed to do before the show.

First, she fixed up and cleaned the theater.

Then, she created all the costumes
that she was going to wear onstage.

She designed and built the sets and all the props.

When everything was ready, she sent out the invitations and put up posters on the buildings around town.

The night before the opening,
Amandina had a marvelous dream.

Opening night came. Amandina was very excited, because she had prepared the show with such care and because of her dream. Of course, she was a little nervous, too. The curtain rose.

The theater was empty: nobody had come.
Sometimes these things happen, and nobody can say why.
Amandina didn't know what to do.

She stood there, as still as a stone. But then she performed. She did everything as planned, starting with a fanciful prologue.

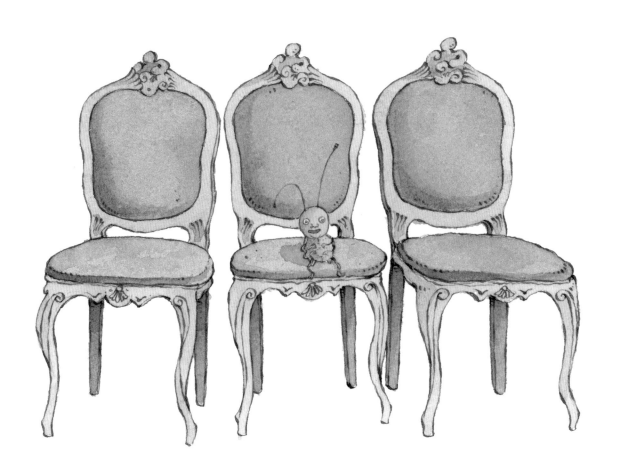

A little cockroach, who was wandering around with no plans for the evening, emerged from a tear in one of the front seats. He was astonished by what he saw!

He called up his friends, who in turn called up their friends.

They were silent, for they were enchanted by the wonderful
show. Amandina didn't even notice that the theater was
now full, as she continued with her program:
A comic pantomime . . .

A shortened version of *Beauty and the Beast* . . .

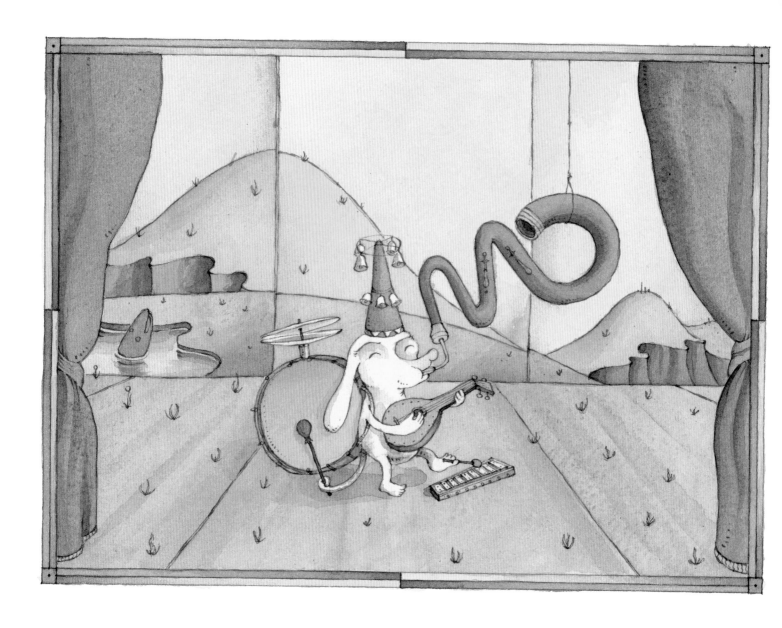

A band concert . . .

Folk songs and dances from all over the world . . .

A magic act . . .

And a stupendous acrobatic feat as a grand finale.

When the show was over, Amandina bowed before what she thought was an empty theater. But when she heard the thunderous applause, Amandina Goldeneyes was the happiest little dog in town.

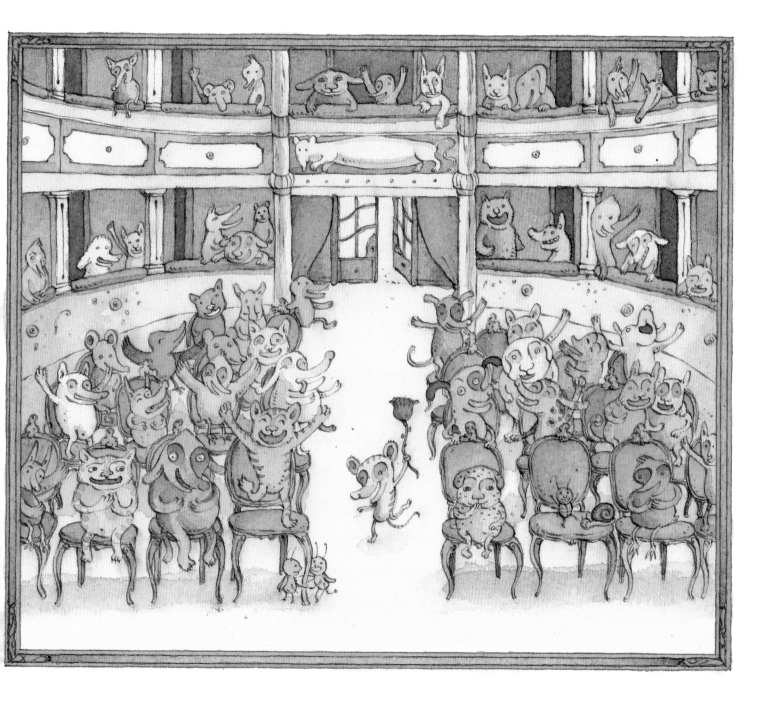